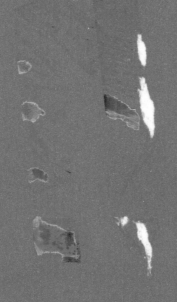

This Book Belongs to

_____

_____

For Bess, thanks for the inspiration.
D.C.

To Glenys and Christopher with love.
R.A.

First published in 2010 by
Gullane Children's Books
185 Fleet Street, London, EC4A 2HS
www.gullanebooks.com

2   4   6   8   10   9   7   5   3   1

Text © David Conway 2010 Illustrations © Roberta Angaramo 2010

The right of David Conway and Roberta Angaramo to be identified as the author and illustrator of this work has been asserted by them in accordance with the Copyright, Designs and Patents Act, 1988.

'Sing a Rainbow' (from 'Pete Kelly's Blues') words and music by Arthur Hamilton
© 1955 (renewed) Mark VII Ltd. All rights administered by WB Music Corp.
All rights reserved. Used by permission of Alfred Publishing Co., Inc.

A CIP record for this title is available from the British Library.

ISBN-978-1-86233-766-4

Printed and bound in Thailand

Errol
and his
Extraordinary Nose

David Conway

illustrated by Roberta Angaramo

GULLANE
CHILDREN'S BOOKS

All of the animals at Acacia Tree Junior School had different
talents and they were always singing their own praises.
"I can swallow almost anything," bragged Abraham the Anaconda.
"If I was running with the herd you would
never spot me," boasted Zachary the Zebra.
"No matter what colour it is, we can change
to match it," gloated the Chameleon Brothers . . .

. . . but none of the animals
thought very much of Errol the
Elephant. They thought he was
awkward and clumsy and that
his nose looked silly.

One day Mr Geoffreys, the Giant Tortoise, made an announcement.
There was to be a talent contest to raise money for the school.

All of the animals were very excited.

All, that is, except Errol.
Everyone will just laugh at me, he thought.

Errol did his very best to
find a talent for the competition.

He tried **juggling,**
but his trunk got in the way . . .

. . . he tried **playing a musical instrument,**
but it sounded just AWFUL!

He even tried **dancing,**
but he was so heavy that he kept on falling over with a great big . . .

By bedtime Errol was feeling very glum.
"I wish I was good at something," he said tearfully.
"There is nothing special about me."
"Now, now," said Errol's dad. "That's not true.
There is something special about everyone.

Everyone has a talent."

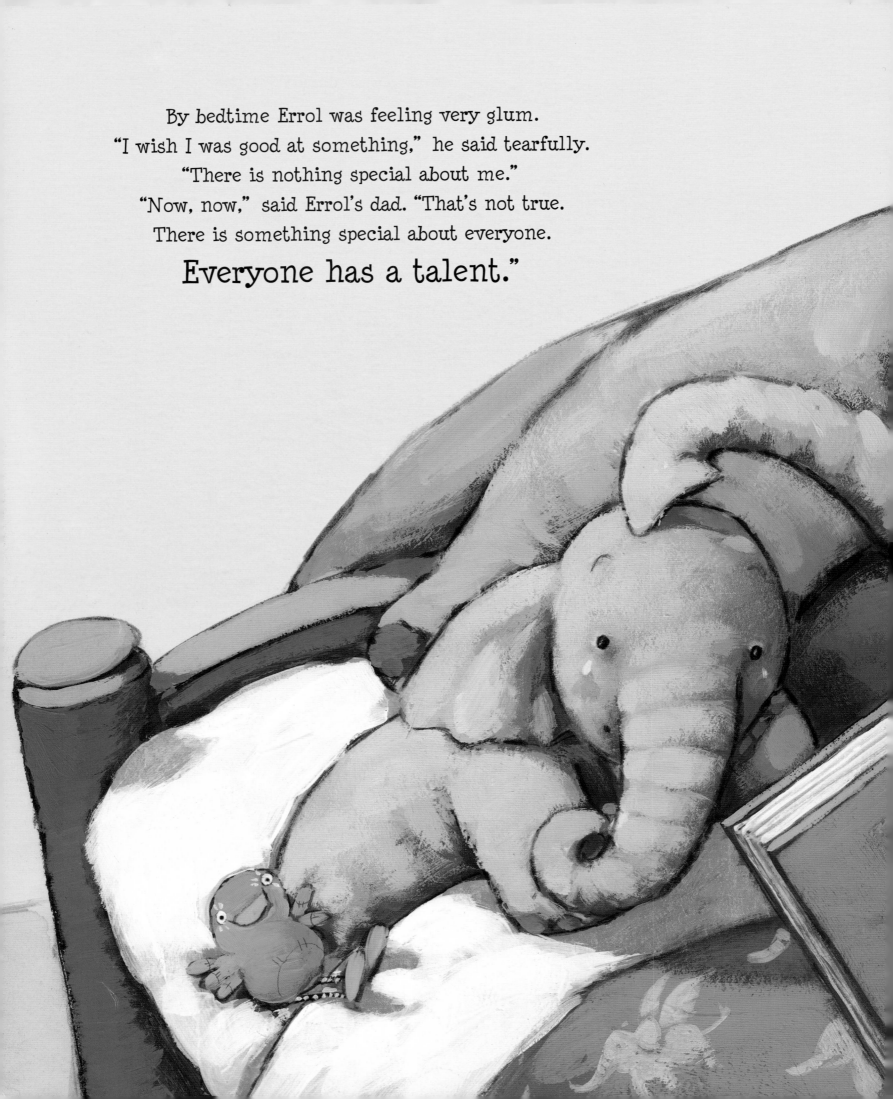

Then his dad gave him a book.
It was a book all about **elephants**.
"If you read this," he said, "you'll
soon see that there are lots of
things that are special about you."

Errol did indeed discover many interesting facts
as he settled down with the book that
evening. Facts like:

Elephants have excellent memories and
elephants can live to a very old age.

But most excitingly, Errol discovered that he was the owner of quite an
extraordinary nose.

It was a nose unlike any other in the animal kingdom,
a very versatile nose. A nose that could be used for · · ·

reaching, and grasping · · ·

spraying, and drinking, and . . .

flinging and flailing, and . . .

snorkelling!

And a nose that could even be used like a periscope for sniffing out smells!

That night Errol felt very different as the dark
cloud that had been hanging over him drifted away.
I have a talent, he thought, *an amazing talent!*
Then he fell into a wonderful, dream-filled sleep.

The day of the talent contest finally
arrived and Errol was feeling a little bit nervous.
But as he peered through a crack in the curtains
he could see his dad in the audience, and
he remembered what he had told him.

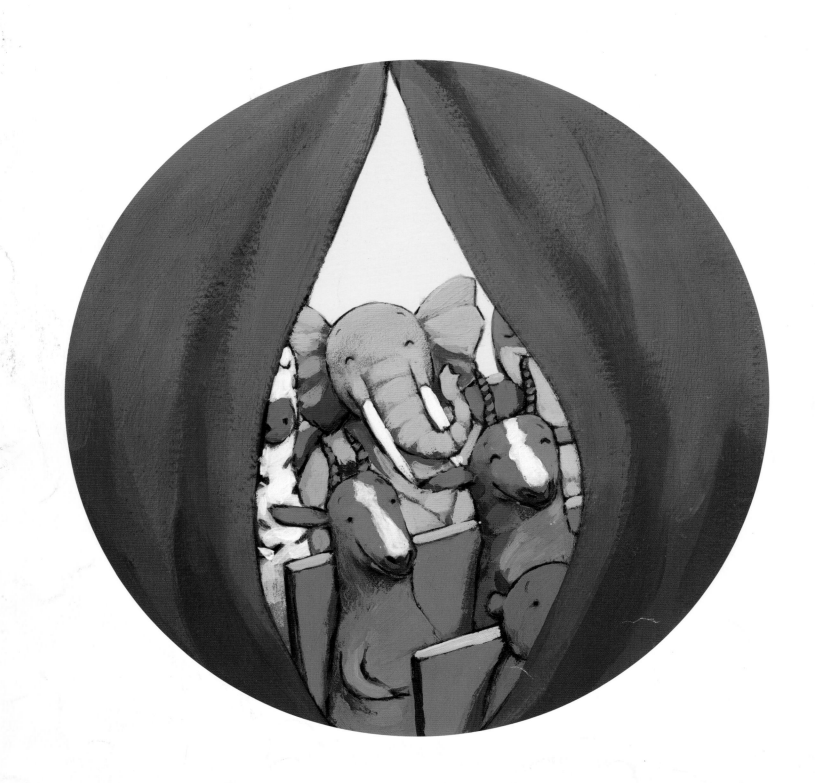

First up were **the Chameleon Brothers** who sang a rendition of
Sing a Rainbow whilst changing into lots of different colours.

Red and yellow and pink and green, purple and orange and blue.
We can sing a rainbow, sing a rainbow, sing a rainbow too . . .

Then . . .

. . . the African Finches sang in a choir . . .

while Morris the Meerkat conducted the orchestra!

Abraham the Anaconda ate two hundred buns . . .

and everyone tried their best to spot Zachary the Zebra.

At last it was Errol's turn to take to the stage.
He was still very nervous, but straightaway he . . .

amazed everyone as he reached
and grasped objects just by using his nose.

And then he . . .

astounded everyone as he danced in
a tank of water whilst using his nose as a snorkelling device.

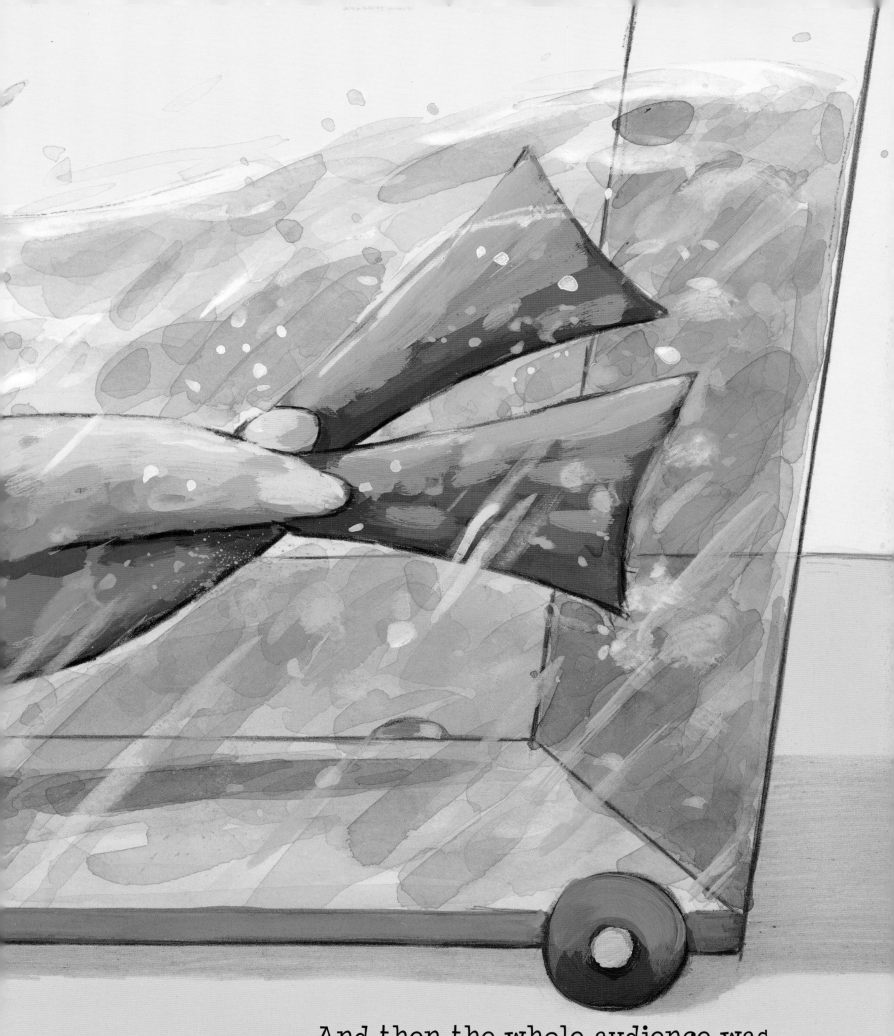

And then the whole audience was . . .

flabbergasted

when Errol created a beautiful
water and light show while singing a
song all about the rain!

When the talent show had finished everyone waited
in anticipation. Third place went to the Chameleon
Brothers for their colourful rendition of the rainbow song.
Second place went to Zachary the Zebra for being very hard to spot.

"And the winner," announced Mr Geoffreys,
"and a well-deserved first place goes to . . .

. . . Errol
and his Extraordinary Nose!"
The whole hall erupted as everyone cheered and clapped.
Errol's dad was so proud of him!

From that day on, none of the other animals at the school thought little of Errol or his nose again. And whenever they ask him how he does the amazing things that he can with his nose, Errol smiles. "There is something special about everyone," he explains . . .

"everyone has a talent!"